MARC BROWN

ARTHUR'S FIRE DRILL

Step into Reading® Sticker Books

Random House 🏠 New York

Copyright © 2000 by Marc Brown. All rights reserved under International and Pan-American Copyright Conventions. Published in the United States by Random House, Inc., New York, and simultaneously in Canada by Random House of Canada Limited, Toronto.

www.randomhouse.com/kids

Library of Congress Cataloging-in-Publication Data
Brown, Marc Tolon. Arthur's fire drill / Marc Brown. p. cm.
SUMMARY: Arthur helps ease D.W.'s fire fear by practicing fire drills at home.
ISBN 0-679-88476-9 (trade) — ISBN 0-679-98476-3 (lib. bdg.)
[1. Fire drills—Fiction. 2. Safety—Fiction. 3. Aardvark—Fiction.]
I. Title. PZ7.B81618Apm 2000 [E]—dc21 99-34964
Printed in the United States of America February 2000 10 9 8 7 6 5 4 3 2 1

STEP INTO READING, RANDOM HOUSE, and the Random House colophon are registered trademarks of Random House, Inc. The Step into Reading colophon is a trademark of Random House, Inc. ARTHUR is a registered trademark of Marc Brown.

When was a
ur taught her
not to touch the hot

"No!" he said. "Hot, hot!"

When D.W. was  years old,
Arthur taught her
about s.
"No," he said.
"Never play with matches!"

Now D.W. is in nursery
Her teacher teaches her
all sorts of things...

how to tie her

how to print her name,

how to share.

1 day the teacher said, "Listen up, and Tomorrow we are going to have a

She told them what to do.
"When the fire 🔔 rings,
stop what you are doing
and quickly line up at the 🚪."

7

Then she took them outside.
"Now stop, drop, and roll
in the  she said.
They all stopped, dropped,
and rolled.

"This is fun!" said D.W.

"But what's it for?"

One of the Tibble twins said

"It's if your clothes catch on

"Oh!" said D.W. in a tiny voice.

That night D.W. whispered to Arthur,
"I'm not going to school tomorrow."
"Why not?" asked Arthur.
"There's going to be a 🔥 she said.
"You're making this up," said Arthur.
"Am NOT!" said D.W.
"Our teacher even
showed us what to do
when we catch fire tomorrow.
Stop! Drop! And roll!"
Arthur had to laugh.
"That's a fire DRILL,"
he said.

"It teaches you what to do
 if there ever is a real fire."
"I don't care what you say," said D.W.
"I'm not going to school tomorrow."

"I have an idea," said Arthur, and he went into his closet. When he came out, he gave D.W. his play firefighter's  and a very loud

"We'll have a fire drill at home,"
said Arthur,
"and you can be in charge."

"Great!" said D.W.
"I get to be the fire boss."
"But first," said Arthur,
"you need to know the rules."

Arthur's Fire Safety Rules

☑ Don't hide. Get outside!

Never go back in.

☑ Stay low and go!

If you have to go through ,

put a wet on your head

and crawl out.

☑ Always use the

Never use the elevator.

☑ Be prepared!

Plan a way out now

with your family.

Always remember to first
get out of your  quickly.

Then go to a neighbor's house
to ne the firehouse.

Just dial 911.

"Okay," said D.W. "I'm ready."
She ran down the stairs.
She blew her whistle. WHEEeee!
"Fire drill! Fire drill! Everyone out!
And don't forget Baby Kate,"
she shouted.

"WHAT!" said Dad.

"Just do what she says,"
said Arthur.

"She is the  boss."

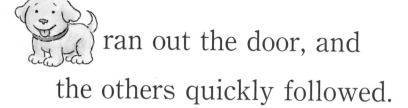 ran out the door, and
the others quickly followed.

"What's all this about?"
asked Dad.

"It's D.W.'s homework,"
said Arthur.

"Tomorrow is her first fire drill."

D.W. had two more fire drills
that night.

"That's enough, D.W.," said Dad.

Then she made Arthur practice
how to get through fire or

"Hey! I'm all wet!"

shouted Arthur. "That's it!"

The next morning
D.W. was ready for school early.
But when she got there,
she saw a big  fire truck
out front.
"Oh, no!" she said.
"The school is on fire!
I need to get everyone out!"

Just then something strange
stepped out of the fire
D.W. took one look at it
and screamed, "Help!
A monster!"

The strange thing said,
"Don't be afraid.
I'm not a monster.
I'm just a friendly firefighter."
And he took off his
"See! This mask helps us
breathe in heavy smoke.
I'm here today to tell your class
how we fight fires.
Shall we go in?"
"I'll help, too,"
said D.W.
"I'm a fire boss."

After school,  asked "How was the fire drill?"

"No big deal," answered D.W.